Cows Can't Spin Silk

By Dave Reisman

Illustrations By Jason A. Maas

JumpingCowPress.com

JUMPING COW PRESS

For my brothers,
Rich, Rob & Dan
With love,

Published by Jumping Cow Press
JumpingCowPress.com

CPSIA Notice
This Second Paperback Edition of "Cows Can't Spin Silk" was manufactured,
printed and bound in December 2017 by Wai Man Book Binding (China)
Limited in Dongguan City, China in full compliance with the United States
Consumer Product Safety Improvement Act

Cows can't spin silk...

...but they can make milk.

Woodpeckers can't make milk...

4

...but they can hammer holes.

Alligators can't
hammer holes...

...but they can dig gator-ponds.

Spiders can't dig
gator-ponds...

...but they can
weave webs.

9

Hens can't weave webs...

...but they can lay eggs.

Skunks can't
lay eggs...

...but they can spray stench.

Ants can't spray
stench...

...but they can build bridges.

Chipmunks can't build bridges...

...but they can bore tunnels.

Bluejays can't bore tunnels...

...but they can
assemble nests.

Caterpillars can't assemble nests...

...but they can
construct cocoons.

Wasps can't construct cocoons...

...but they can craft paper.

Beavers can't craft paper...

...but they can form dams.

...but they can shape tools.

Squids can't shape tools... ✒

...but they can squirt ink.

29

Oysters can't squirt ink...

...but they can produce pearls.

Octopuses can't produce pearls...

...but they can erect barricades.

Bees can't erect
barricades...

...but they can
create honey.

Bears can't
create honey...

...but they can make dens.

Visit the Jumping Cow Press website for our shop,
free printable learning resources and more!

www.jumpingcowpress.com

Available in Paperback, Stubby & Stout™
and eBook Formats

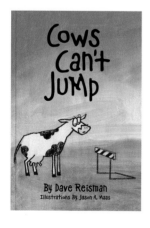 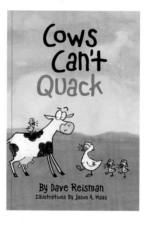